The Chord boyzone

Wise Publications
London/New York/Paris/Sydney/Copenhagen/Madrid

Exclusive Distributors:
Music Sales Limited
8/9 Frith Street,
London W1V 5TZ, England.
Music Sales Pty Limited
120 Rothschild Avenue,
Rosebery, NSW 2018, Australia.

Order No. AM956956
ISBN 0-7119-7304-0
This book © Copyright 1999 by Wise Publications

Music arranged by Rikky Rooksby
Music processed by The Pitts

Cover design by Pearce Marchbank, Studio Twenty

Printed in the United Kingdom by
Caligraving Limited, Thetford, Nolfolk.

Your Guarantee of Quality
As publishers, we strive to produce every book
to the highest commercial standards.
This book has been carefully designed to minimise awkward
page turns and to make playing from it a real pleasure.
Particular care has been given to specifying acid-free,
neutral-sized paper made from pulps which have not been
elemental chlorine bleached. This pulp is from farmed sustainable
forests and was produced with special regard for the environment.
Throughout, the printing and binding have been planned to
ensure a sturdy, attractive publication which should give years
of enjoyment. If your copy fails to meet our high standards,
please inform us and we will gladly replace it.

Music Sales' complete catalogue describes thousands
of titles and is available in full colour sections by subject,
direct from Music Sales Limited. Please state your areas of interest
and send a cheque/postal order for £1.50 for postage to:
Music Sales Limited, Newmarket Road,
Bury St. Edmunds, Suffolk IP33 3YB.

www.musicinprint.com

Relative Tuning

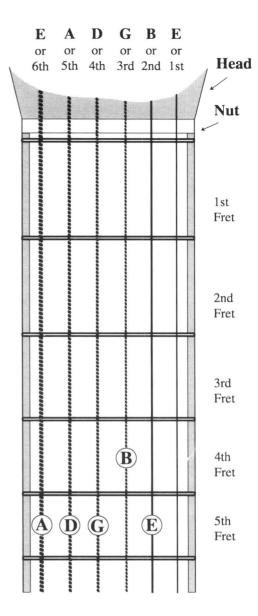

The guitar can be tuned with the aid of pitch pipes or dedicated electronic guitar tuners which are available through your local music dealer. If you do not have a tuning device, you can use relative tuning. Estimate the pitch of the 6th string as near as possible to E or at least a comfortable pitch (not too high, as you might break other strings in tuning up). Then, while checking the various positions on the diagram, place a finger from your left hand on the:

5th fret of the E or 6th string and **tune the open A** (or 5th string) to the note Ⓐ

5th fret of the A or 5th string and **tune the open D** (or 4th string) to the note Ⓓ

5th fret of the D or 4th string and **tune the open G** (or 3rd string) to the note Ⓖ

4th fret of the G or 3rd string and **tune the open B** (or 2nd string) to the note Ⓑ

5th fret of the B or 2nd string and **tune the open E** (or 1st string) to the note Ⓔ

Reading Chord Boxes

Chord boxes are diagrams of the guitar neck viewed head upwards, face on as illustrated. The top horizontal line is the nut, unless a higher fret number is indicated, the others are the frets.

The vertical lines are the strings, starting from E (or 6th) on the left to E (or 1st) on the right.

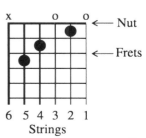

The black dots indicate where to place your fingers.

Strings marked with an O are played open, not fretted.

Strings marked with an X should not be played.

3

A Different Beat

Words & Music by Martin Brannigan, Stephen Gately,
Ronan Keating, Shane Lynch & Ray Hedges

Tune down a semitone

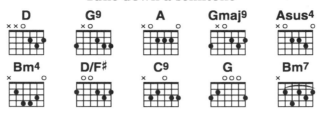

Intro (drums)

Verse 1

D
Let's not forget this place,

G9
Let's not neglect our race,

D
Let unity become

A
Life on earth be one.

D
So let me take your hand,

Gmaj9
We are but grains of sand

D
Born through the winds of time

Asus4   **A**
Given a special sign.

Prechorus 1

Gmaj9
So let's take a stand

A
And look around us now, people

Gmaj9
So let's take a stand

A
And look around us now, people.

Chorus 1

D   **G⁹**   **Bm⁴**   **A**
Eeyeya-oh, eeyea-oh, eeyea-oh, by-yah.

          D
To a different beat

         G⁹   **Bm⁴**   **A**
Eeyea-oh, eeyea-oh, eeyea-oh, by-ya

Verse 2

        D
Humanity's lost face

        G⁹
Let's understand its grace.

        D
Each day one at a time,

        A⁴   **A**
Each life including mine.

Prechorus 2

      Gmaj⁹
So let's take a stand

               A
And look around us now, people.

      Gmaj⁹
So let's take a stand

               A
And look around us now, people.

Oh people, oh people.

Chorus 2   As Chorus 1

Bridge

D/F♯   **G**   **A** **Bm7**
I've seen the rain fall in Africa (Africa),_____

D/F♯   **G**   **A**
I've touched the snows of Alaska,

(Oh tell me now)

D/F♯   **G**   **A** **Bm7**
I've felt the mists of Niagara,

          C9   **D**
Now I believe in you.

Chorus 3   As Chorus 1

Chorus 4   (chant continues)

D   **G9**
How far we've come

Bm4   **A**
And how far to go.

D   **G9**
Rain does not fall

Bm4   **A**   **G9** **D**
On one roof alone._____

All That I Need

Words & Music by Evan Rogers & Carl Sturken

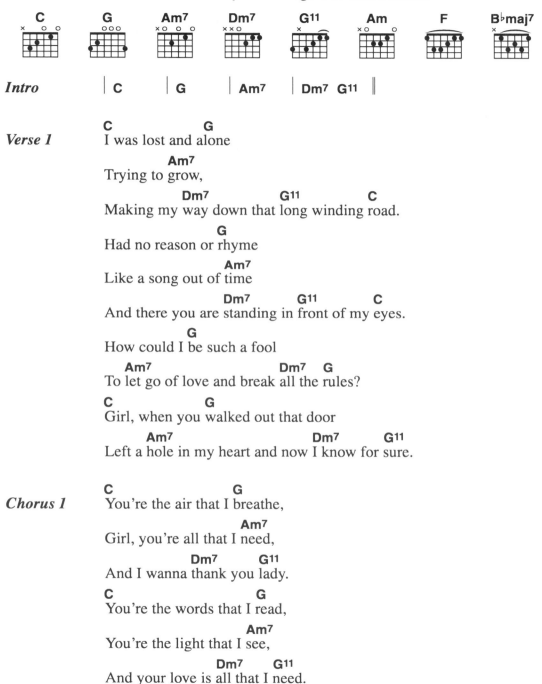

Intro | C | G | Am⁷ | Dm⁷ G¹¹ ‖

Verse 1

C   G
I was lost and alone

Am⁷
Trying to grow,

Dm⁷   G¹¹   C
Making my way down that long winding road.

G
Had no reason or rhyme

Am⁷
Like a song out of time

Dm⁷   G¹¹   C
And there you are standing in front of my eyes.

G
How could I be such a fool

Am⁷   Dm⁷ G
To let go of love and break all the rules?

C   G
Girl, when you walked out that door

Am⁷   Dm⁷   G¹¹
Left a hole in my heart and now I know for sure.

Chorus 1

C   G
You're the air that I breathe,

Am⁷
Girl, you're all that I need,

Dm⁷   G¹¹
And I wanna thank you lady.

C   G
You're the words that I read,

Am⁷
You're the light that I see,

Dm⁷   G¹¹
And your love is all that I need.

Link | C | G | Am7 | Dm7   G11 ‖

Verse 2
> C   G
> I was searching in vain,
>
>   Am7
> Playing your game
>
>   Dm7   G11   C
> Had no-one else but myself left to blame.
>
>   G
> You came into my world,
>
>   Am7
> No diamonds or pearls
>
>   Dm7   G11   C
> Could ever replace what you gave to me, girl.

Prechorus 2
> C   G
> Just like a castle of sand,
>
>   Am7
> Girl, I almost let love
>
>   Dm7   G
> Slip right out of my hand.
>
> C   G
> And just like a flower needs rain
>
>   Am7
> I will stand by your side
>
>   Dm7   G11
> Through the joy and the pain.

Chorus 2

C   G
You're the air that I breathe,

        Am7
Girl, you're all that I need,

      Dm7 G11
And I wanna thank you lady

C   G
you're the words that I read,

        Am7
You're the light that I see

      Dm7 G11
And your love is all that I need.

Instr. Solo | Am | F | B♭maj7 | Dm7 G11 ‖

Chorus 3 As Chorus 1

Coda

C   G
You're the song that I sing,

        Am7
Girl, you're my everything

      Dm7 G11
And I wanna thank you lady.

C
You're all that I needed, girl,

G
You're the air that I breathe, yeah

Am7   Dm7 G11
And I wanna thank you, lady. *Repeat to fade*

9

Arms Of Mary

Words & Music by Iain Sutherland

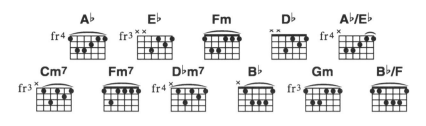

Intro | A♭ | ‖

Verse 1
A♭   E♭
The lights shine down the valley,
Fm   D♭
The wind blows up the alley,
A♭/E♭
Oh, and how I wish I was
E♭   A♭
Lying in the arms of Mary.

Verse 2
A♭   E♭
She took the pains of boyhood
Fm   D♭
And turned them into feel good,
A♭/E♭
Oh, and how I wish I was
E♭   A♭
Lying in the arms of Mary.

Bridge
                    Cm7   Fm7
Mary was the girl who taught me all I had to know,
                    D♭   E♭
She put me right on my first mistake.
                    Cm7   Fm7
Summer wasn't gone when I'd learned all she had to show
                    D♭   E♭
She really gave all a boy could take.

Verse 3

A♭   E♭
So now when I feel lonely

Fm   D♭
Still looking for the one and only,

A♭/E♭
That's when I wish I was

E♭   A♭ D♭m7
Lying in the arms of Mary.

Verse 4   As Verse 3

Link

| A♭ | E♭ | | Fm | D♭ | |
Mary

| A♭/E♭ | E♭ | | A♭ | ‖
Mary   (Mary was the…)

Bridge 2 As Bridge 1

Verse 5

B♭   F
The lights shine down the valley,

Gm   E♭
The wind blows up the alley,

B♭/F
Oh, and how I wish I was

F   Gm
Lying in the arms of Mary.

Coda

E♭   F Gm
Lying in the arms of Mary.

E♭   F Gm
Lying in the arms of Mary

       E♭ F
Yeah, yeah, yeah, yeah_____

Gm   E♭ F
Lying in the arms

Gm   E♭ F
Lying in the arms *to fade*

Baby Can I Hold You?

Words & Music by Tracy Chapman

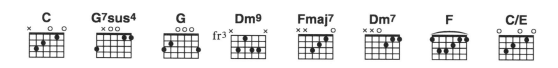

Intro | C | G⁷sus⁴ G | C | G⁷sus⁴ G ‖

Verse 1

C   G⁷sus⁴ G   Dm⁹
Sorry is all that you can't say.

G⁷sus⁴   G   C
Years gone by and still

G⁷sus⁴   G   Dm⁹
Words don't come easily

Fmaj⁷   G
Like sorry, like sorry.

Verse 2

C   G⁷sus⁴ G   Dm⁹
Forgive me is all that you can't say.

G⁷sus⁴   G   C
Years gone by and still

G⁷sus⁴   G   Dm⁹
Words don't come easily

Fmaj⁷   G
Like forgive me, forgive me.

Chorus 1

           C
But you can say "Baby,

Dm⁷   F   C
Baby can I hold you tonight?

Dm⁷   F   Am
Baby if I told you the right words,

         G
Ooh, at the right time

         C
You'd be mine."

Link | Dm   C/E   F   G   ‖

Verse 3

C   **G7sus4 G**   **Dm9**
"I love you" is all that you can't say

G7sus4   **G**   **C**
Years gone by and still

G7sus4   **G**   **Dm9**
Words don't come easily

             Fmaj7   **G**
Like "I love you, I love you."

Chorus 2   As Chorus 1

Chorus 3

Dm7   **F**   **C**
"Baby can I hold you tonight?

Dm7   **F**   **Am**
Baby, if I told you the right words,

            G
Ooh, at the right time

            C
You'd be mine".

C   **Dm7 F**
(Baby, if I told you, baby can I hold you?)

Coda   **C**
                                     you'd be mine

C   **Dm7 F**
(Baby, if I told you, baby can I hold you?)

                             C
                                     you'd be mine

C   **Dm7**
(Baby, if I told you)

F   **C**
Baby, can I hold you?

13

Coming Home Now

Words & Music by Stephen Gately, Ronan Keating,
Michael Graham, Shane Lynch & Keith Duffy

Fmaj9/C Cmaj9 Fmaj7 Em7 Cmaj7 Gsus4

Intro | Fmaj9/C | Cmaj9 | Fmaj9/C | Cmaj9 ‖

(Spoken)

Fmaj9/C   Cmaj9
Weeks, days, hours, minutes till I'll be home

Fmaj9/C   Cmaj9
Weeks, days, hours, minutes till I'll be home

Fmaj9/C   Cmaj9
Da-da da da da-da, da-da da da da-da

Fmaj9/C   Cmaj9
Da-da da da da-da, da-da da da da-da.

Verse 1

Fma79/C
A kiss on the cheek in the old town park,

Cmaj9
Carved your name in the shape of a heart

Fmaj9/C
Walked together hand in hand.

Cmaj9   Fmaj9/C   Cmaj9
I didn't feel the rain.

Fmaj7

Prechorus 1   And there's a picture girl,

Em7

That hangs inside my mind

Fmaj7

And there's a letter girl

Cmaj7 Em7

Say I'm doing fine.

Fmaj7

And there's a picture, girl

Em7

That hangs inside my mind

Fmaj7

And there's a letter girl

G4

Say I'm doing fine.

Fmaj9/C

Chorus 1   And I'm coming home now

Cmaj9

It's been so long now,

Fmaj9/C

Gonna get there somehow

Cmaj7

Praying you'll be there.

Fmaj9/C

Coming home now,

Cmaj9

It's been so long now,

Fmaj9/C

Gonna get there somehow,

Cmaj9

Praying you'll be there.

N.C.

Link   Weeks, days, till I'll be there.

Verse 2

Fmaj9/C
Children on the streets

Still playing their games,
Cmaj9   **Fmaj9/C**
The smiles on their faces have never changed
                    Cmaj9 Fmaj9/C
I hope it's all the same,
                    Cmaj9
I didn't leave in vain.

Prechorus 2   As Prechorus 1

Chorus 2   As Chorus 1

**Verse 3
(Spoken)**

Fmaj7
"Dearly close words: I really want to see you.
Em7
You're in my heart when overseas.
  Fmaj7
I feel you close, and not so far.

                        G4
Soon we'll be together, and this time it's forever."

Chorus 3   And I'm coming home now

It's been so long now,

Gonna get there somehow

Praying you'll be there.

Chorus 4   As Chorus 1

Father And Son

Words & Music by Cat Stevens

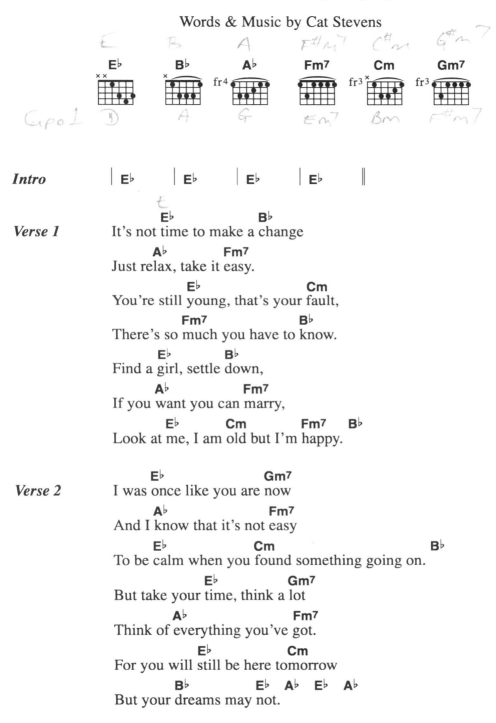

Intro | Eb | Eb | Eb | Eb ||

Verse 1

         Eb   Bb
It's not time to make a change
          Ab   Fm7
Just relax, take it easy.
              Eb   Cm
You're still young, that's your fault,
          Fm7   Bb
There's so much you have to know.
            Eb   Bb
Find a girl, settle down,
          Ab   Fm7
If you want you can marry,
            Eb   Cm   Fm7 Bb
Look at me, I am old but I'm happy.

Verse 2

         Eb   Gm7
I was once like you are now
          Ab   Fm7
And I know that it's not easy
         Eb   Cm   Bb
To be calm when you found something going on.
             Eb   Gm7
But take your time, think a lot
           Ab   Fm7
Think of everything you've got.
              Eb   Cm
For you will still be here tomorrow
         Bb   Eb Ab Eb Ab
But your dreams may not.

Verse 3

E♭   Gm7
How can I try to explain?

      A♭   Fm7
When I do he turns away again;

      E♭   Cm   Fm7 B♭
Well, it's always been the same, same old story.

      E♭   Gm7
From the moment I could talk

    A♭   Fm7
I was ordered to listen,

      E♭   Cm
Now there's a way and I know

    B♭   E♭
That I have to go away.

B♭   A♭   E♭ A♭ E♭ A♭
I know I have to go.

Verse 4

      E♭   B♭
It's not time to make a change

    A♭   Fm7
Just sit down and take it slowly

     E♭   Cm
You're still young, that's your fault

    Fm7   B♭
There's so much you have to go through.

     E♭   Gm7
Find a girl, settle down

    A♭   Fm7
If you want you can marry

     E♭   Cm   Fm7 B♭
Look at me, I am old but I'm happy.

Verse 5

       E♭   Gm7
All the times that I've cried

          A♭   Fm7
Keeping all the things I know inside;

       E♭   Cm7   Fm7   B♭
And it's hard, but it's harder to ignore it.

           E♭   Gm7
If they were right I'd agree

         A♭   Fm7
But it's them they know not me;

            E♭   Cm
Now there's a way, and I know

     B♭   E♭
That I have to go away.

B♭   A♭   E♭
I know I have to go.

I Love The Way You Love Me

Words & Music by Chuck Cannon & Victoria Shaw

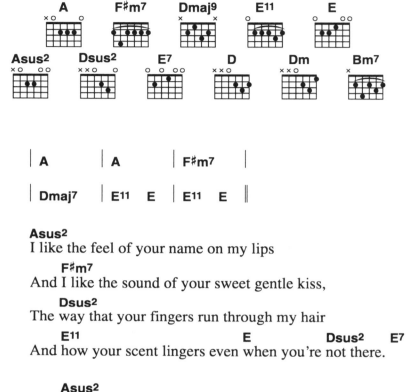

Intro | A | A | F♯m7 |

| Dmaj7 | E11 E | E11 E ‖

Verse 1

Asus2
I like the feel of your name on my lips

F♯m7
And I like the sound of your sweet gentle kiss,

Dsus2
The way that your fingers run through my hair

E11   **E**   **Dsus2** **E7**
And how your scent lingers even when you're not there.

Verse 2

Asus2
And I like the way your eyes dance when you laugh

F♯m7
And how you'll enjoy your two-hour bath

Dsus2
And how you convinced me to dance in the rain

E11   **E**   **E11**   **E**
With ev'ryone watchin' like we were insane.

Chorus 1

Dmaj9 **E7**   **A**
But I love   the way you love me, oh baby

Dmaj9   **E7**
Strong and wild, slow and easy,

A   **D**
Heart and soul, so completely.

E11   **A**   **Dm** **E7**
I love the way you love me, yeah.

Verse 3

           G
And I like the sound of old R and B

           G
You roll your eyes when I'm slightly off key

G
And I like the innocent way that you cry

G
From sappy old movies you've seen thousands of times.

Chorus 2

Dmaj9 **E7**   **A**
But I love   the way you love me, oh baby

Dmaj9   **E7**
Strong and wild, slow and easy,

A   **D**
Heart and soul, so completely,

E11   **A**
I love the way you love me.

Bridge
$$E$$
(So listen to me now)

D   **E**
And I could list a million things

A
I'd love to like about you (about you).

D   **A**
But they all come down to one reason,

Bm7   **E11**   **E7**
I could never live without you.

Chorus 3
Dmaj9 E7   **A**
I love   the way you love me, oh baby

Dmaj9   **E7**
Strong and wild, slow and easy,

A   **D**
Heart and soul, so completely,

E11   **A**   **E   G   D**
I love the way you love me.

Coda
Dsus2 E11   **Asus2**
I love   the way that you love me.

22

Isn't It A Wonder?

Words & Music by Martin Brannigan, Ronan Keating & Ray Hedges

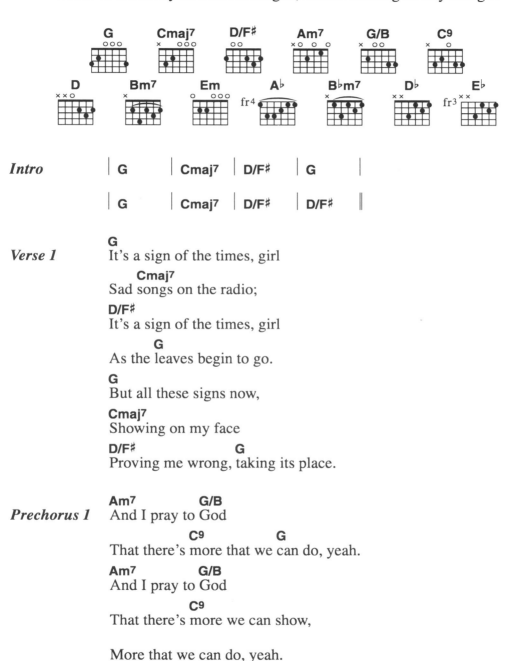

Intro　　| G　　| Cmaj7　| D/F♯　| G　　　|

　　　　　　| G　　| Cmaj7　| D/F♯　| D/F♯　‖

Verse 1

G
It's a sign of the times, girl

　　　Cmaj7
Sad songs on the radio;

D/F♯
It's a sign of the times, girl

　　　　　G
As the leaves begin to go.

G
But all these signs now,

Cmaj7
Showing on my face

D/F♯　　　　　　　**G**
Proving me wrong, taking its place.

Prechorus 1

Am7　　　　　**G/B**
And I pray to God

　　　　　　　　C9　　　　　**G**
That there's more that we can do, yeah.

Am7　　　　　**G/B**
And I pray to God

　　　　　　　C9
That there's more we can show,

More that we can do, yeah.

Chorus 1

```
G        Am7         C              D
Isn't it a wonder, as a new-born baby cries,
G            Am7           C                D
And isn't it a wonder with the sweetness in my eyes,
G        Am7           C              D
Isn't it a wonder, on the crossroads of my life
Am7              D                  G
Isn't it a wonder, isn't it a wonder to me?
```

Link

```
Am7  C  D  G      Am7  D
Oh oh oh, yoh oh oh.
```

Verse 2

```
G
It's the way of the world when
Cmaj7
Wrong takes hold of right,
D/F#
It's the way of the world,
    G
In which we've all lost sight
G                    Cmaj7
But isn't this world too simple to be true?
D/F#          G
Holding on to memories of you.
```

Prechorus 2   As Prechorus 1

Chorus 2

```
G        Am7         C              D
Isn't it a wonder, as a newborn baby cries,
G            Am7           C                D
And isn't it a wonder with the sweetness in my eyes.
G        Am7           C              D
Isn't it a wonder, at the crossroads of my life
Am7              D
Isn't it a wonder, isn't it a wonder?
```

Verse 3

       C9   **G/B**
That I can see a change in me

      C9   **G**
But I won't go back 'cause that's behind me.

      C9   **Bm7**   **Em**
And after all strong words are spoken

F9
My heart will never be, never be, never be, never be…

Chorus 3

  A♭   **B♭m7**   **D♭**   **E♭**
Isn't it a wonder, as a new-born baby cries,

  A♭   **B♭m7**   **D♭**   **E♭**
And isn't it a wonder with the sweetness in my eyes,

  A♭   **B♭m7**   **D♭**   **E♭**
Isn't it a wonder, at the crossroads of my life,

B♭m7   **E♭**
Isn't it a wonder, isn't it a wonder?

Chorus 4

      A♭   **B♭m7 D♭**   **E♭**
That I can see a change in me

      A♭   **B♭m7**   **D♭**   **E♭**
But I won't go back 'cause that's behind me.

    A♭ **B♭m7 D♭**   **E♭**
And after all strong words are spoken

B♭m7   **E♭**
My heart will never be, never be, never be, never be.

Instr coda | **A♭** **B♭m7** | **D♭** **E♭** | **A♭**   ‖

Key To My Life

Words & Music by Martin Brannigan, Stephen Gately,
Ronan Keating, Michael Graham & Ray Hedges

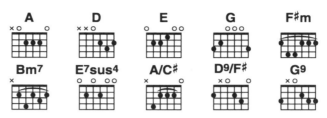

Intro | A D | E A ||

D   E   G
You're the key to my life

Verse 1

A
Rain on the window covers the trace

F♯m
Of all the tears that I've had to waste,

Bm⁷
And now I'm missing you so

          A   E⁷sus⁴
And I won't let you go away.

Verse 2

A
Stain on the desktop where coffee cup lay

F♯m
And memories of you forever will stay

Bm⁷
And the scent of your perfume,

         A
And the smile of your face will remain.

Prechorus 1

              D   E
And I never gave up hope when things got me down

      D
But I just bit on my lip

        E   A
And my face began to frown.

A/C# D
'Cause that was just my pride

        E
And I've nothing left to hide,

   Bm7
And now the way is clear

   E
And all I want to say is:

Chorus 1

A   D   E   A
All of my life the doors have been closed now,

    F#m   Bm7   E   A
And all of my dreams have been locked up inside.

           D   E   A
But you came along and captured my heart, girl,

D   E   G   D9/F#   A
You're the key to my life ---------- yea-ah.

Verse 3

A
Year after year, was blaming myself

F#m
For what I'd done; just thought of myself.

        Bm7
I know that you'll understand

                           A
This was all my own fault – don't go away.

Prechorus 2   As Prechorus 1

Chorus 2

```
        A        D     E              A
All of my life the doors have been closed now,
        F♯m    Bm               E        A
And all of my dreams have been locked up inside.
        A         D      E            A
But you came along and captured my heart, girl,
D        E        G
You're the key to my life.
```

(Girl)

Bridge

```
G9
Girl, you know that I feel for you
A
There ain't nothing that I wouldn't do,
G9
Stop the thunder and the pouring rain,
D          A
You're the one that's gonna stop the pain.
G9
Girl, you know that I feel for you,
A
There ain't nothing that I wouldn't do.
D
Stop the thunder and the pouring rain –
E
Listen to me, can't you hear what I say?
```

Chorus 3

```
        A        D     E              A
All of my life the doors have been closed now,
        F♯m      Bm              E        A
And all of my dreams have been locked up inside.
        A         D      E            A
But you came along and captured my heart, girl.
D        E        G        D9/F♯   A
You're the key to my life ----    yea-ah.
```

Love Me For A Reason

Words & Music by John Bristol, Wade Brown Jr & David Jones Jr

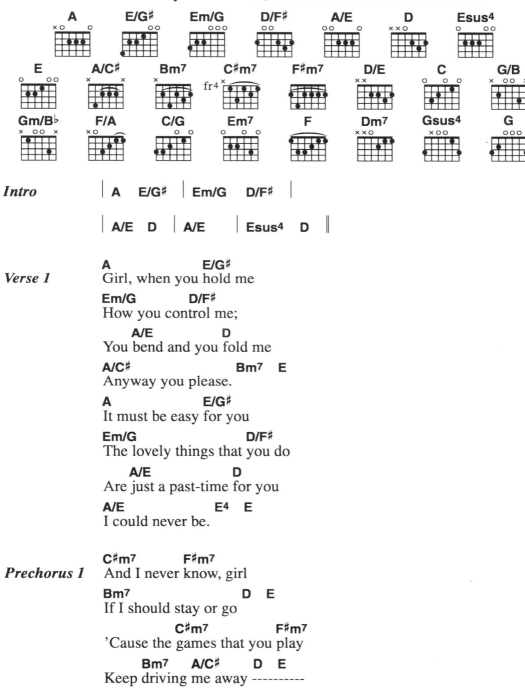

Intro | A E/G♯ | Em/G D/F♯ |

| A/E D | A/E | Esus⁴ D ‖

Verse 1

A   E/G♯
Girl, when you hold me

Em/G   D/F♯
How you control me;

     A/E   D
You bend and you fold me

A/C♯   Bm⁷ E
Anyway you please.

A   E/G♯
It must be easy for you

Em/G   D/F♯
The lovely things that you do

   A/E   D
Are just a past-time for you

A/E   E⁴ E
I could never be.

Prechorus 1

C♯m⁷   F♯m⁷
And I never know, girl

Bm⁷   D E
If I should stay or go

       C♯m⁷   F♯m⁷
'Cause the games that you play

     Bm⁷ A/C♯   D E
Keep driving me away ----------

Chorus 1

A   C#m7
Don't love me for fun, girl,

D   A
Let me be the one, girl,

Bm7   A/C#
Love me for a reason,

D   E4   E
Let the reason be love.

Chorus 2

A   C#m7
Don't love me for fun, girl,

D   A
Let me be the one, girl,

Bm7   A/C#
Love me for a reason,

D   E
Let the reason be (love)

Link

| A | D/E A   D | A/E Esus4   E ‖
love

Verse 2

A   E/G#
Kisses and caresses

Em/G   D/F#
Are only minor tests, babe

   A/E   D
Of love needs and stresses

A/C#   Bm7 E
Between a woman and a man.

A   E/G#
So if love everlasting

Em/G   D/F#
Isn't what you're asking,

A/C#   Bm7
I'll have to pass, girl;

A/E   E4   E
I'm proud to take a stand.

Prechorus 2

C♯m7   F♯m7
I can't continue guessing,

Bm7   D   E
Because it's only messing

        C♯m7   F♯m7
With my pride and my mind.

   Bm7   A/C♯ D   E
So write down this time to time;

Chorus 3   As Chorus 1

Chorus 4   As Chorus 2

Link | C   G/B | Gm/B♭ F/A | C/G F | Esus4   E ‖

Prechorus 3

C♯m7   F♯m7
I'm just a little old-fashioned:

Bm7   D   E
It takes more than a physical attraction,

C♯m7   F♯m7   Bm7   A/C♯
My initial reaction is, "Honey, give me love;

       D   E
Not a facsimile of."

Chorus 5   As Chorus 1

Chorus 6   As Chorus 2 (no chords) (a capella)

Chorus 7

C   Em7
Don't love me for fun girl,

F   C
Let me be the one, girl,

Dm7   C
Love me for a reason,

F   Gsus4 G
Let the reason be love.

Chorus 8   As Chorus 7   *to fade*

Picture Of You

Words & Music by Eliot Kennedy, Ronan Keating,
Paul Wilson & Andy Watkins

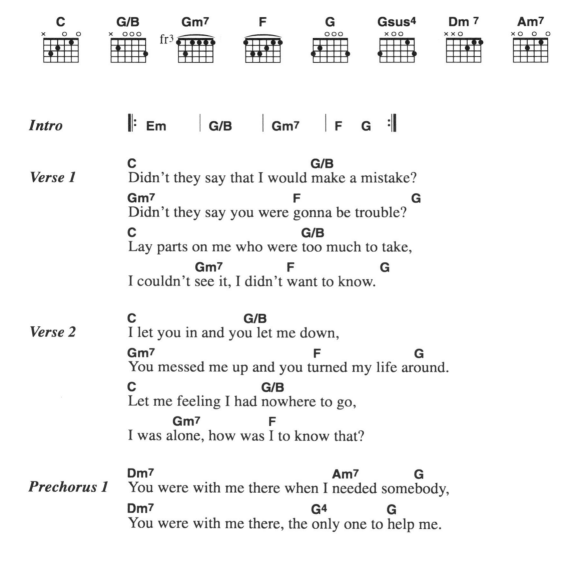

Intro   ‖: Em | G/B | Gm⁷ | F   G :‖

Verse 1

  C   G/B

Didn't they say that I would make a mistake?

Gm⁷   **F**   **G**

Didn't they say you were gonna be trouble?

C   **G/B**

Lay parts on me who were too much to take,

           Gm⁷   **F**   **G**

I couldn't see it, I didn't want to know.

Verse 2

  C   **G/B**

I let you in and you let me down,

Gm⁷   **F**   **G**

You messed me up and you turned my life around.

C   **G/B**

Let me feeling I had nowhere to go,

     Gm⁷   **F**

I was alone, how was I to know that?

Prechorus 1

Dm⁷   **Am⁷**   **G**

You were with me there when I needed somebody,

Dm⁷   **G⁴**   **G**

You were with me there, the only one to help me.

Chorus 1

```
   C      G/B                   Gm7
```
I had a picture of you in my mind,
```
         F              G C
```
Never knew it could be so wrong.
```
          G/B                   Gm7
```
Why'd it take me so long just to find
```
           F                 G
```
The friend that was there all a(long.)

Link

| C | G/B | Gm7 | F G ‖

- long.

Verse 3

```
   C                          G/B
```
Do you believe that after all that we've been through
```
Gm7          F           G C
```
I'd be able to put my trust in you?
```
                             G/B
```
Goes to show you can forgive and forget
```
           Gm7    F
```
Looking back I have no regrets, 'cause

Prechorus 2   As Prechorus 1

Chorus 2   As Chorus 1

Instr

| C | G/B | Gm7 | F G |

- long.

| C | G/B | Gm7 | F ‖

Prechorus 3

```
Dm7                        Am7          G
```
You were with me there when I needed somebody,
```
Dm7                      G4          G
```
You were with me there, the only one to help me ____

Chorus 3   As Chorus 1 (twice)

Chorus 4   As Chorus 1 *to fade.*

No Matter What

Music by Andrew Lloyd Webber
Lyrics by Jim Steinman

Chord diagrams: A, A7, D, Bm, Bm/A, Esus4, E, A/C#

C, Dm, Gsus4, G, Dm7, C7/E, C/E, Am7

Intro

| A | A7 | D | D |
| D | D | Bm | A ‖

Verse 1

  A
No matter what they tell us,
          Bm/A
No matter what they do,
Bm   **Esus4** **E**
No matter what they teach us,
Esus4 **E**   **A**
What we believe is true.

Verse 2

  A
No matter what they call us,
          Bm/A
However they attack,
Bm   **Esus4** **E**
No matter where they take us,
Esus4 **E**   **A**
We'll find our own way back.

Chorus 1

  A   **A7**
I can't deny what I believe,
D   **A/C#**
I can't be what I'm not,
Bm   **Esus4 E**
I know our love's forev - er
Esus4 **E**   **A**
I know no matter what.

Verse 3

     A
If only tears were laughter,
              Bm/A
If only night was day
Bm   **Esus⁴**   **E**
If only prayers were answered
Esus⁴   **E**   **A**
Then we would hear God say.

Verse 4

     A
No matter what they tell you,
              Bm/A
No matter what they do,
Bm   **Esus⁴ E**
No matter what they teach   you,
Esus⁴   **E**   **A**
What you believe is true.

Chorus 2

     A   **A⁷**
And I will keep you safe and strong,
        D   **A/C♯**
And sheltered from the storm.
Bm   **Esus⁴ E**
No matter where it's bar - ren
Esus⁴   **E**   **A**
Our dream is being born.

Instr

| | C | | C | | C | | Dm | |
| **Dm** | | **Gsus⁴ G** | **Gsus⁴ G** | **C** | ‖ |

Verse 5

     C
No matter who they follow,
             Dm⁷
No matter where they lead,
Dm   **Gsus⁴**   **G**
No matter how they judge us,
Gsus⁴   **G**   **C**
I'll be everyone you need.

Chorus 3

C   C7/E
No matter if the sun don't shine

F   C/E
Or if the skies are blue,

Dm   Gsus4   G
No matter what the end - ing

Gsus4   G   C
My life began with you.

Chorus 4

C   C7/E
I can't deny what I believe,

F   C/E
I can't be what I'm not.

Dm   Gsus4   G
I know this love's forever

Gsus4   G   C
That's all that matters now

         C   Am7
No matter what.

Coda

G   C   Am7
No, no matter what

G   C   Am7
No, no matter what

C
No, no matter,

Am7   G   C
That's all that matters to me. *Repeat to fade*

So Good

Words & Music by Martin Brannigan, Stephen Gately, Ronan Keating,
Michael Graham, Shane Lynch, Keith Duffy & Ray Hedges

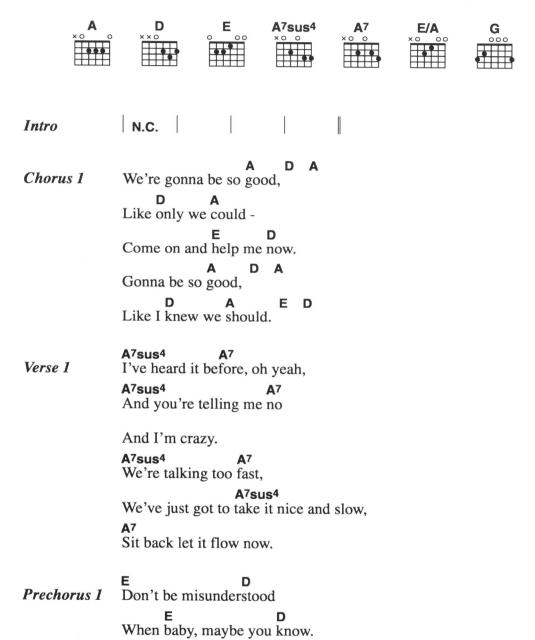

Intro | N.C. | | | ‖

Chorus 1

                     A   **D** **A**
We're gonna be so good,

       D   **A**
Like only we could -

            E   **D**
Come on and help me now.

         A   **D** **A**
Gonna be so good,

       D   **A**   **E** **D**
Like I knew we should.

Verse 1

A⁷sus⁴   **A⁷**
I've heard it before, oh yeah,

A⁷sus⁴   **A⁷**
And you're telling me no

And I'm crazy.

A⁷sus⁴   **A⁷**
We're talking too fast,

                A⁷sus⁴
We've just got to take it nice and slow,

A⁷
Sit back let it flow now.

Prechorus 1

    E   **D**
Don't be misunderstood

       E   **D**
When baby, maybe you know.

Chorus 2

              A
We're gonna be so good,

     D   **A**
Like I knew we would,

    D   **A**
Like only we could -

          E   **D**
Come on and help me now.

          A
Gonna be so good,

     D   **A**
'Cause it's understood,

    D   **A**
Like I knew we should.

       E   **D**
Hi - - - - hah, so good now baby.

Link 1

A⁷sus⁴ **A⁷**
    (We're gonna be so good)

A⁷sus⁴ **A⁷**
    (Don't you know that we could be good)

Verse 2

A⁷sus⁴   **A⁷**
No matter the cost, oh yeah

A⁷sus⁴   **A⁷**
When we're out on the town

Getting lazy.

A⁷sus⁴   **A⁷**
I'll show you who's boss,

           A⁷sus⁴
We're just gonna take it all the way

  A⁷
No matter what they say now.

Prechorus 2   As Prechorus 1

Chorus 3   As Chorus 2

Link 2 ‖ A E/A | A E/A | A E/A | A E/A ‖

   A E/A
(Be so good)

A   E/A
Be so good, now.

  A E/A
(Be so good).

Prechorus 3   As Prechorus 1

               A
Chorus 4   We're gonna be so good,

      D   A
Like I knew we would,

     D   A
Like only we could -

         E   D
Come on and help me now.

        A
Gonna be so good,

      D   A
'Cause it's understood,

      D   A
Like I knew we should.

      E D
Hi - - - - ha.

     E   D A
Coda   We're gonna be so good,

      D   A
Like I knew we would,

     D   G
You know we're good.

This Is Where I Belong

Words & Music by Evan Rogers, Carl Sturken & Ronan Keating

Tune down a semitone

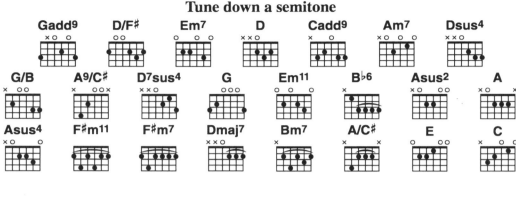

Intro | Gadd 9   D/F♯ | Em7   D | Cadd9 |

Verse 1

Gadd9   D/F♯   Em7
Here I stand in the northern rain

        Am7   Em7
And I can't believe I'm home again.

        Am7   Em7
And I can't believe how nothing's changed,

        D   Dsus4   G   G
I'm finding   my   way.

Verse 2

Gadd9   D/F♯   Em7
Old park bench on where I carved my name

        Am7   Em7
But now it doesn't stand all alone

          Am7   Em7
'Cause now the trees have overgrown

D/F♯   G   Am7
Ma - ny a road that I've travelled

          G/B
That's led me astray,

Cadd9   A9/C♯   D7sus4
Here's where my heart's gonna stay.

Chorus 1

Gadd9   G   Gadd9   G
This is where I be - long,

Em11   Em7   Em11
This is where I come from,

Em7   Cadd9
No need to shed my tears

G/B   Am7   D7sus4
Or face my fears anymore, oh____

Gadd9   G   Gadd9   G
So I won't walk   alone,

Em11   Em7   Em11
Taking things on my own.

Em7   Cadd9
All of the lands I've roamed,

G/B   B♭6
Mem'ries of my home, they keep beating strong

D7sus4   Gadd9   G   Gadd9   G
'Cause this is where I be - long.

Verse 3

Gadd9   D/F♯ Em7
There you stood in the open door

Am7   Em7
Just like so many years before.

Am7   Em7 D G C9
When I told you that I needed more in my life.

Gadd9   D/F♯   Em7
I was wrong to ever walk away

Am7   Em7
Abandon all the love that we made

Am7   Em7
But now I've learned from all my mistakes

D/F♯ G   Am7   G/B
Just   like a star in the sky guiding me on

Cadd9   A9/C♯   D7sus4
Your love is pulling me home.

Chorus 2   As Chorus 1

Link
```
| Gadd 9   G  | Gadd 9   G  | Gadd9     ‖
```
G   **Am7**
Just like a star in the sky

G/B
Guiding me on

Cadd9   **A9/C♯**   **D7sus4**
Your love is pulling me home.

              Asus2 A Asus4 A
Chorus 3   This is where I be - long,

                F♯m11 F♯m7 F♯m11
This is where I come from,

F♯m7   **Dmaj7**
No need to shed my tears

  A/C♯   **Bm7**   **E11**
Or face my fears anymore, oh _____

      Asus2 A Asus2 A
So I won't walk alone,

          F♯m11 F♯m7 F♯m11
Taking things on my own,

F♯m7   **Dmaj7**
All of the lands I've roamed,

      A/C♯   **C**   **E11**
Mem'ries of my home, they keep beating strong

          Asus2 A
'Cause this is where I be - long.

Coda

Asus2 A F#m11   F#m7   F#m11

Right here, right now,

        F#m7   Asus2 A Asus2 A

Baby this is where I belong

    F#m11   F#m7   F#m11 F#m7

I'm coming home, I'm coming home_____

              Asus2 A

This is where I be - long

 Asus2   A

(Na-na na na-na na na)

 F#m11   F#m7

(Na-na na na-na na na)

  F#m

(Na-na na na-na na na)

 F#m7   Asus2 A

(This is where I be - long).

          Asus2 A   F#m11 F#m7 F#m11

Here I stand in the northern rain_____

F#m7   Asus2 A

This is where I be - long

Asus2   A   F#m11

(Na-na na na-na na na)

      F#m7   F#m11

Right here, right now

 F#m7   A   Asus2

(This is where I be - long)

 Asus2   A

(Na-na na na na-na na)

 F#m11   F#m7

(Na-na na na-na na na)

 F#m11

(Na-na na na-na)

F#m7   A

This is where I be - long_____

When All Is Said And Done

Words & Music by Martin Brannigan, Stephen Gately, Ronan Keating,
Michael Graham, Shane Lynch, Keith Duffy & Ray Hedges

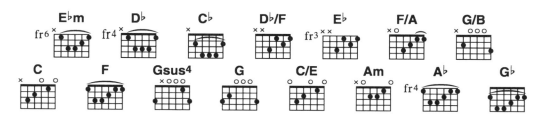

Intro | E♭m | D♭ | C♭ | D♭ ‖

Verse 1
E♭m   D♭
Days that we spent when I was so small -
C♭   D♭
Never let me fall, you never let me fall.
E♭m   D♭
Taught me to see the right and the wrong.
C♭   D♭
Oh, I'm not that strong, wish I was that strong.

Prechorus 1
E♭m   D♭
You've been good to me,
                          C♭
Tending to my every need.
E♭m   D♭
Just look what I am
D♭/F   E♭   F/A   G/B
Can't you see it's you in me?

	C F
Chorus 1	When all is said and done

	C Gsus4 G
	Look before you I'm your son.

	C/E F G Am G
	Can't you see it's you in me?

	F
	A man.

Link 1 | A♭ | G♭ |

	E♭m D♭
Verse 2	Now I'm a man, time has gone fast -

	C♭ D♭
	I didn't want it to, I didn't want it to.

	E♭m D♭
	Went on my way like a crazy young fool -

	C♭ D♭
	I never wanted to, I never wanted to.

Prechorus 2   As Prechorus 1

Chorus 2   As Chorus 1

Instr coda | F | C | F   G |

| C | F   G | C   ‖

Words

Words & Music by Barry Gibb, Robin Gibb & Maurice Gibb

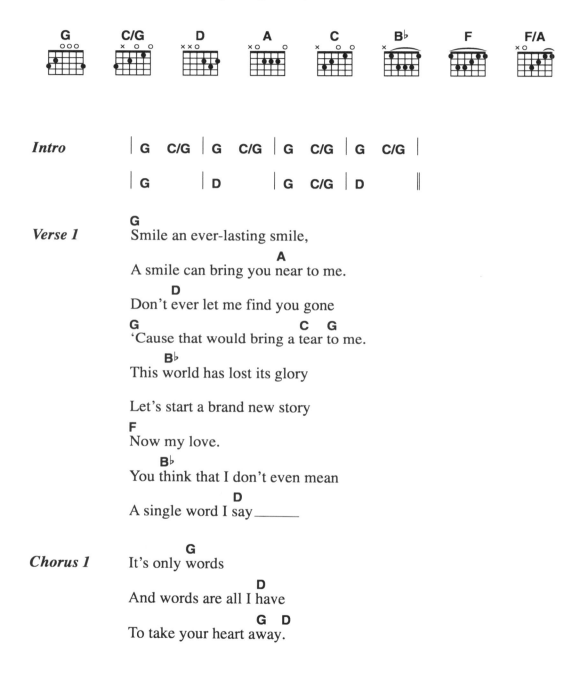

Intro
| G C/G | G C/G | G C/G | G C/G |
| G | D | G C/G | D |

Verse 1

G
Smile an ever-lasting smile,

　　　　　　　　　　　A
A smile can bring you near to me.

　　　　　D
Don't ever let me find you gone

G　　　　　　　　　　**C** **G**
'Cause that would bring a tear to me.

　　　　　　　B♭
This world has lost its glory

Let's start a brand new story

F
Now my love.

　　　B♭
You think that I don't even mean

　　　　　　　　　D
A single word I say _____

Chorus 1

　　　　　　G
It's only words

　　　　　　　　　D
And words are all I have

　　　　　　　　　G D
To take your heart away.

Verse 2   **G**
Talk in everlasting words

             A
And dedicate them all to me,

   D
And I will give you all my life -

          C **G**
I'm here if you should call to me.

    B♭
You think that I don't even mean

          D
A single word I say_____

Chorus 2   As Chorus 1

Chorus 3   As Chorus 1

           G
Bridge   Da da da-da da da da

Da da da-da da da da

A
Da da da

D
Da da da-da da da da

Da da da-da da da da

C **G**
Da da da

Verse 3
F/A   B♭
This world has lost its glory,

Let's start a brand new story
F
Now my love.
    B♭
You think I don't even mean
        D
A single word I say_____

Chorus 4   As Chorus 1

Chorus 5   As Chorus 1

           G
Chorus 6   It's only words
            D
And words are all I have
           G
To take your heart a(way.)

Instr coda | **G   C/G** | **G   C/G** | **G   C/G** | **G**   ‖
- way.